CON

About the Author   iv
New Non-Fiction By Laura Mariani   vi
Also By Laura Mariani   vii

PARIS TOUJOURS PARIS

Quote   5
Prologue   7
Paris Toujours Paris   9

ME MYSELF AND US

Quote   35
Me Myself and Us   37
Afterword   55

FREEDOM OVER ME

Freedom Over Me   59
The greatest love of all   77
Disclaimer   78
Author's Note   79

THE NINE LIVES OF GABRIELLE: FOR THREE, SHE STRAYS

BOOK 1-3 COLLECTION

LAURA MARIANI

The
PEOPLE
ALCHEMIST

ABOUT THE AUTHOR

Laura Mariani is an Author, Speaker and Entrepreneur.

She started her consulting business after a successful career as Senior HR Director within global brands in FMCG, Retail, Media and Pharma.

Laura is incredibly passionate about helping other women to break through barriers limiting their personal and/or professional fulfilment.

Her best selling nonfiction *STOP IT! It is all in your head* and the *THINK, LOOK & ACT THE PART* series have been described as success and transformation 101.

She is a Fellow of the Chartered Institute of Personnel & Development (FCIPD), Fellow of the Australian Human Resources Institute (FAHRI), Fellow of the Institute of Leadership & Management (FInstLM), Member of the Society of Human Resources Management (SHRM) and Member of the Change Institute.

She is based in London, England with a strong penchant for travel and visiting new places. She is a food lover, ballet fanatic, passionate about music, art, theatre. She likes painting and drawing (for self-expression not selling but hey, you never know…), tennis, rugby, and of course fashion (the Pope is Catholic after all).

www.thepeoplealchemist.com
@PeopleAlchemist
instagram.com/lauramariani_author

NEW NON-FICTION BY LAURA MARIANI

ALSO BY LAURA MARIANI

Fiction

For Three She Plays - Book 1 - 3

A New York Adventure

Troubled after the break-up of a long term relationship, Gabrielle sets out for a sabbatical in New York.

A travelogue searching for self, pleasure and fun. And the Big Apple doesn't disappoint.

Searching for Goren

Why are we always choosing people who don't allow intimacy? Is it because deep down we don't want it?

Tasting Freedom

As her trip to New York comes to an end, her shackles bare falling and Gabrielle begins to taste, finally, freedom.

Non-Fiction

STOP IT! It is all in your head

The RULE BOOK to Smash The infamous glass ceiling -

For women & young women everywhere - personal transformation & success 101.

The Think, Look & Act The Part Series.

Think The Part

Upgrade your consciousness and mind-set.

Make winning a key part of your life and business.

Look The Part

Upgrade your personal brand.

Make presenting your unique Best Self a key part of your life and business.

Act The Part

A personal coach to act in spite of fear, right here, right now.

More non-fiction books and courses are coming soon.

For new releases, giveaways and pre-release specials check www. thepeoplealchemist.com

You can also buy my books and courses directly from me at www. payhip.com/LauraMariani

ThePeopleAlchemist Press publishes self help, inspirational and transformational books, resources and products to help #TheWomanAlchemist in every woman to change her life/career and transmute any circumstance into gold, a bit like magic to **Unlock Ignite Transform.**

ISBN: 978-1-915501-08-0

Paris Toujours Paris

THE NINE LIVES OF GABRIELLE: FOR
THREE SHE STRAYS - BOOK 1

LAURA MARIANI

To Paris, one of my three loves

"PARIS IS ALWAYS A GOOD IDEA"
- **AUDREY HEPBURN**

PROLOGUE

S elf-Image is our self-limiting portable box.
Our world and everything in it reflects our mental attitude toward ourselves.

It's the ultimate internal regulator: whenever the temperature rises above comfort level, it will take us back to base like a thermostat. Self-image is determined by the paradigms that run our life and mind unconsciously.

Unless we resolve our deep-rooted issues, address our core needs and then up-level our self-image, we will reach the "temperature" we are comfortable in sooner or later. Then Self-sabotage comes in.

And there we start again.

And sometimes, we cross the line and our moral compass to meet our needs.

Laura xxx

G abrielle woke up, the sun filtering through the gap in the heavy curtains.

They were back home after a long weekend celebrating. Celebrating in more ways than one.

The day before, after dinner and the night at the Opera, Gabrielle had finally started to open up to Mr Wonderful. They were out to celebrate the day they met—another of the many surprises from Mr Wonderful.

He was still asleep, and she couldn't stop looking at him, fearing he would disappear like a *mirage.* How lucky she was.

And how afraid she was going to screw this up too.

Mr Wonderful lips were slightly arched as if whatever he was dreaming of made him smile. His thick dark eyebrows were framing his masculine face perfectly. A strand of hair covering his forehead and just a little stubble from a few days without shaving covering his face. He smelled soo good: a mixture of his cologne and after-sex pheromones. His arms were still around her, as he couldn't quite sleep without being close to her, skin to skin.

He was very handsome and, from his facial expressions, looked like he was having a perfect dream.

Gabrielle was lying there, motionless, trying not to breathe, not to wake him up. Precious moments. She loved them and savoured them. No questions asked. Just contemplating how lucky she was. Especially after talking, aka talking about herself. They spent the previous day talking, or at least it had felt like a day to Gabrielle.

She had to.

She had spent the whole time whilst they were at dinner and the Opera wondering in and out of her consciousness, back and forward from her past. And he had noticed. Of course.

He was always so attentive. "Too much sometimes", thought Gabrielle. She'd prefer if he couldn't read her so well. What she had always craved was here, and it was not as easy as she had hoped. Intimacy is a bummer.

She always liked to present the best of herself. The best of herself she wanted the world to see. Being laid bare was excruciating.

"Good morning, gorgeous",

Mr Wonderful said, flashing one of his dazzling smiles. Perfect pearly whites. His blue eyes pierced through her soul.

"Good morning",

She purred and sunk her face into his chest, trying not to look into his eyes. He knew she had done enough talking, at least for now, far more than she was used to, so he held her firmly, stroking her back whilst kissing her forehead.

"I love you",

Mr Wonderful whispered, "Always".

Gabrielle looked up for a minute and replied,
" I love you too, more than I can say".
"I know".

They stayed in bed some more, lingering.
The crumpled bed sheets around them.

After some time had passed, she got up and started getting ready for her morning walk. One of the few habits she developed during lockdown that she kept after starting her relationship with Mr Wonderful. You can't exactly run an overnight tape with 'I am a Goddess' affirmations when you are sleeping next to someone you are remotely interested in— or can't sleep either with one of those gizmos with Bluetooth, still not very sexy.

But she kept the morning walks and writing her morning pages. She started carrying a notebook with her on her walks and stopped from time to time to write her thoughts. Whatever came to mind: anything and everything.

Mr Wonderful was a gym type of person, so she used that time to do her own thing.

"Darling, I need to write some papers for work. Do you mind if I use your office?" he asked.

Ever so polite, he understood how precious Gabrielle was with her space, house, and things. Between falling deeply in love and lockdown, they practically moved in together almost immediately, and he was wary of not "overstepping" and being overfamiliar. He was determined not to take anything for granted.

"Not going to the gym?" Gabrielle asked.
    "Maybe after I finish work, I have a deadline".
    "Sure, I am going for a walk".
    "I'll be here", Mr Wonderful replied.

Gabrielle always enjoyed walking, especially down the canal. Being near the water, the sounds and the smell made her feel at peace and relaxed. She often stopped and sat to write her morning pages whilst watching the canal and the locals going on with their daily life. The water was standing still...

"Be still and know that I...," peacefully meditating in the moment.

The door closed behind Gabrielle, and Mr Wonderful jumped out of bed and into a quick shower before getting ready to do some work.

With a fresh cup of coffee in his hand, he then proceeded towards the small crook in the corner of the house that Gabrielle had designated as an office. There it was where Gabrielle did all her work, painting, writing and filming for her YouTube channel. A foldable antique lacquered screen was concealing the area.

. . .

Clear boundaries, "So Gabrielle," he thought as he folded the screen away and sat at the desk.

He powered up his laptop, checked his emails and then the stock exchange, followed by a quick call to his broker to sell and buy some stock and shares. The desk was just by the window, looking over Canonbury Square and Canonbury Gardens.

He found himself wondering.
   Wondering how hard he had fallen for her and how fast.

How she walked into his life out of the blue. He had never met anybody before this enchanting, enthralling, and so elusive.

His previous long-term relationships had always played the second field to his business and personal interests: cars, racing, and flying. And now, all he wanted was Gabrielle.

Her big brown eyes had captivated him from the first moment; her perfume seduced him, and her voice sealed the deal.

But, most of all, it was her sweetness and vulnerability hiding behind the strong, badass facade.

· · ·

Yes, she was beautiful, almost hypnotising, even more, because she was playing it down and self-deprecating. She didn't fully realise the effect she had on men, or on him. When she walked into a room ...

"Boy, I have fallen hard," he thought.

"I need paper. Where does she keep printing paper?" he asked himself.

He looked into a few drawers of Gabrielle's exquisite French cabinet which she used as a desk.

"Nope", pens, highlighters, pencils, brushes but no paper. "Ah, here it is," he said as he opened the last drawer.

As he took the A4 paper out of the drawer, he noticed something that looked like a folded note. Maybe something Gabrielle had written recently ...

"I shouldn't look", he thought, reminding himself how private she was.

But the letter bated, called him and tempted him to read it. For hours he resisted and kept on working. But he couldn't concentrate, he was distracted. The letter kept popping into his mind.

Then, finally, he gave in; he made another cup of coffee, sat down and unfolded the inviting note.

"*Ma chérie Gabrielle, n'aie pas peur de combien je te désire*".

. . .

Mr Wonderful French was rusty, but he understood a few core words like "*désire*". He searched for Google Translate on his laptop and typed the words with apprehension.

"Dear Gabrielle, don't be afraid of how much I desire you", read the first line.

His heart was sinking, and his mind was going awry.
"When was it written? Where is the date? There is no date in this letter," he thought.

He cursed himself for not paying more attention to the French classes in school and not practising more French with Gabrielle. The process of translating phrase by phrase was excruciatingly painful. So slow. Mr Wonderful's mind was playing with his heart when he noticed that Gabrielle was standing right there, looking at him looking at her, the letter unfolded in his hands.

Gabrielle couldn't help but notice his expression, the colour had drained from his face.

Gone was the loving look he had earlier on. Instead, Mr Wonderful looked stone-faced, almost grey; his eyes were red and swollen.

"Has he been crying?" she thought. "What is he reading?".

It was then she noticed the open drawer where she kept THE letter. *Le PDG* wrote it to her when he feared that their love affair was doomed to end, and soon.

Paris, Toujours, Paris taunting her.

After the New York sabbatical, Gabrielle felt reinvigorated with a new perspective on life. In the last month in the Big Apple, she had thoroughly worked on herself and done some introspection.

Gabrielle had always shied away from getting too deep into anything: relationships, herself, life. She never understood how she always stopped on the verge of greatness, on the brink of enormous success.

Something always happened, somehow, and she couldn't see the pattern. But now, everything looked so painfully clear. Too painful. Gabrielle had so many shields and layers that she wasn't just protecting herself from the world. She was keeping herself from the world.

Back in London, in familiar places, everything however looked so different. She remembered escaping from her "village" and arriving in London only to confine herself to another "village", barely getting out of it. A self-imposed upgraded cage, which now was feeling claustrophobic.

Gabrielle was back at work and ready for new challenges. Work had always been her safe place, where her achievements spoke for themselves with her identity firmly rooted in them. Work had been her life.

Her phone rang.
"Did you have a good time?"
Her MD asked.
"Yes, thanks, fabulous!"
She replied.
"Are you going all American on me now?"
He smirked. "Can I see when you have a minute?".
"Sure, I have a gap in my schedule after lunch. Sheryl has already planned my life for the next decade",
Gabrielle said.
"Yes, your P.A. is very efficient. After lunch, it is fine".

Gabrielle caught up with emails and read the summary prepared for her. Sheryl had been sifting through her emails while Gabrielle was away and diverting them to the appropriate member of her team.

"What would I do without my Sheryl?" she said.

After looking at the latest report on market share and preparing for the meetings in the afternoon, Gabrielle took some time for lunch. She could have easily met the MD over that hour, but her P.A. had made a point of blocking time so she could take care of herself, eat properly and not just gulp something down whilst talking about work. She was behaving more like her mother every day.

• • •

Knock, knock...

"Come in", the MD said. "Coffee?".

"Yes, please," said Gabrielle.

"When you were in New York, lots of changes happened, some moves, some people left", he started, clearing his throat.

"Yes, I know; Sheryl has filled me in. I have seen the announcement for the departure. Interesting", she replied.

"Usual announcement in this type of case", implying this particular one hadn't been a 'voluntary' leaver.

"Well, with all these changes", he proceeded, "there are now empty positions, you know ... opportunities", looking at Gabrielle intensely.

"I imagine so", she said. The penny hadn't dropped yet.

"What's going on with you?" he asked. "What happened in New York? You would have knocked at my door. Hell, putting it down to talk to me about opportunities before".

She squinted her eyes.

"Well, never mind. There is a permanent position opening in Paris, working with the main Board of Directors for the Group and *Le PDG* But the role is based in France. What do you think?"

Gabrielle was happy to be back at work and in her element but, for once in her life, she hadn't quite thought or planned her next move. At least not yet.

"I love Paris. It sounds interesting. I just bought my house in London",

She said tentatively, thinking a permanent move to France was not exactly what she had anticipated.

"You know the company helps with relocation, finding a place and so on..."

"Yes, I know".

"So, what do you think?" he repeated.

Gabrielle knew that if you truly wanted to advance your career in the company, you had to both go and handle the acquisition and integration of a new company into the Group, the French way, and have worked in France. At least for a bit.

They were the unspoken rules. Paired with the other unspoken rule that all company directors throughout the Group have to speak French.

Although English was the commercial language of the Group, if you met *Le PDG* or present to him and the Board, you did so in French.

"If you are interested, they are interviewing next week in Paris. First, second and third interview on the same day".

"Validating?" she kind of asked, but not really.

"Yes, that's right. Validating".

Gabrielle knew French working culture well and the politics that come with that. It was the differentiating factor that got her job role: that and the fact she was bilingual. Gabrielle was working as Marketing and PR Director for the Group branch in the UK, the not-so-unspoken rebel.

. . .

France wanted the UK branch to be managed the French way, but the UK was having none of it. They needed an in-betweener to bridge the cultural gap.

"Why don't you leave then? "

Gabrielle said during a UK board meeting to one of her colleagues, the Sales Director.

Everybody turned to look at her, astonished that she had said that aloud.

The Sales Director was a middle-aged Scottish man who had worked for the company for twenty years; ten before the company was acquired by the French Group.

In ten years, despite lessons, he still couldn't string two French sentences together. Gabrielle had lost her (French) patience with him.

He was not feeling appreciated, blah blah blah ... the French this, blah blah... the French that, blah blah blah...

"If you don't like it, why don't you leave?"

She repeated.

"In this day and age, companies should recognise their employees", he kept on moaning.

"You are not an employee. You are a Board Director. And that's not the culture! This is a French company. More direct, *combative* and with far less sugar coating.

You are expected to do well. It is a bit like school and parents going to meet their children's teacher to find out how they are doing. The teacher will not sing the child's praises and tell the gushing mother how wonderful the child is.

Non, the teacher will point out what the child is not doing well. Because they are expected to do well within the confinements of their age group. Same as you are expected to do well in a job you get paid handsomely to do. You are not going to get praised for it too. Get over it".

They all looked at her like she had just made a significant revelation.

"Sorry all, but that's the way it is."

Gabrielle was so French when in London and so British when in France.

Politics and all the sycophants that worked with *Le PDG* was something she would need to get used to pretty fast.

The Group Board of Directors was a mix of old schoolmates of *Le PDG* or people who had risen through the ranks from when his father was at the company's reign.

He had grown the company from a small artisan one in the north of France to one of the most prominent in the country, and now, *Le PDG* had expanded it globally, acquiring an average of one or two companies per year, every year.

· · ·

Gabrielle was presenting for the first time to *Le PDG* in her new capacity and wanted to make an impression.

She had researched the subject thoroughly and prepared stats and figures to back up her proposed strategy. Her presentation was in English, but all the handouts were in French, and she presented in French. She dressed up for the occasion, too: more feminine than she would have in London but pared down, letting her mind do the talking.

The office was in *Tour Montparnasse* with a spectacular view of the *Tour Eiffel*. The room was set up in a traditional presentation style with *Le PDG* placed right in the middle of the table, his right-hand and left-hand men on each side, and then in order of importance and inner circle closeness. He was known in the company for asking many questions; the unspoken rule to anyone presenting to him was 'know your figures or suffer the consequences'.

"A bit dramatic", she thought, but she memorised all the figures and handouts nevertheless. Just in case.

Le PDG was in his early forties and had been leading the company for at least ten years, the sole shareholder of a private now multi-billion euros company.

He was tall and slender, wearing tortoise glasses resting on his long aquiline nose. His hair was mousy, with a hint of grey running through his temples.

. . .

He was notoriously private, so much so that there weren't any pictures of him in circulation, much to the dismay of the French press.

His anonymity allowed him to travel between *Londrienne* and Paris on the TGV on his own, unnoticed.

Le PDG looked at Gabrielle intensely as she entered the room. Gabrielle had sent copies of her presentation and collateral in advance and expected a grilling.

And she got one.

He interrogated her for hours, the only one asking the questions. All the others nodded, making the obligatory "*Oui, oui*" noises from time to time.

Gabrielle stood there, defiant, answering every question without hesitating. She had memorised every page and every figure and tried to pre-empty every question he might have. It was a duel — a hypnotic duet they were playing. His eyes never once left hers.

Penetrating hers.

And at the end "*Bon*". And the meeting was over.

As everyone started to get up and leave the room, he said:
"We are going for lunch now. Would you like to join us?".

· · ·

Gabrielle wondered if this happened all the time, but this wasn't the time for questioning. "*Oui, merci,*" she said.

They all left and went down the elevator for what seemed like an eternity.

The company office was based on the 55th floor, just below the observation deck on the 56th and the rooftop garden on the 59th. *Le PDG* was standing right next to her, towering over her. He was intent on conversing with one of the others, but she could feel the warmth of his body.

The descent went slowly, with a stop on almost every floor. And with more people coming in, the lift was feeling more and more snuggling. *Le PDG* closer and closer.

As they walked out of the building, he started walking beside her and making small talk nonchalantly. Next, they went to one of the restaurants in the area for lunch. He sat next to her and then talked with everyone around the table but Gabrielle.

She did the same.

As they were all chatting, their arms touched, at first, occasionally and unintentionally.

Then, as the lunch went on, more and more. Gabrielle looked around to see if anyone at the table was paying attention, but they all seemed oblivious and immersed in the food experience.

When back in the office, Gabrielle composed herself in the ladies' room.

"What are you doing? He is THE boss, and he is married",

She said, looking into the mirror.

"Nothing, I'm doing nothing. It was only lunch. It meant nothing".

But it did. It meant something indeed. Things capitulated from there.

The next time they met was at a tasting for a new product line. A room full of people, but they could only see each other. They were inevitably drawn to one another, each trying to overcome their fallacies and the incongruences the situation posed to both.

Gabrielle still remembered what it felt like finding out she was the other woman with the Stud. She felt physically sick.

And *Le PDG* was a good catholic boy who had been married to his childhood sweetheart for the last twenty years. He was living in Paris, Mondays to Fridays, and travelling back to *Londrienne* to spend the weekend with his wife and their three children.

Paris was not for her, the wife; she had lived in her small town all her life and had never wanted to leave. Paris was too much for her.

· · ·

She enjoyed the quiet life, meeting with her friends for lunch whilst the children were at school. He was her security and validation.

Everyone in town, in one way or another, was connected to her husband's company, and she revelled in that.

He always wanted to travel and conquer the world, and his work allowed him just that. And he did take the world by storm; nobody believed he could carry the company when his father died, let alone make it a global multi-billion euros one. So he married young because it was expected to do; their families intertwined. And she was a good wife. Better still, she was loyal and invisible.

Gabrielle, on the other hand, was everything he wanted. She was equally driven, pushing herself all the time.

He wanted her but wasn't one hundred per cent sure she would reciprocate. He thought all the signs were there, but she was a puzzle.

Gabrielle was equally attracted, like the moth to the fire but wasn't quite sure he wanted her enough to do anything about it. And he was married.

So they played their dance, sussing each other out, a life argentine tango.

And then one day, everything changed.

. . .

"Hello Madame, *Le PDG* wants to go through the new strategy and the budget; he has an opening tomorrow at 4.00 pm", his Executive Assistant said over the phone.

"I'll have to move a meeting", Gabrielle said.

"Please do", she replied.

Gabrielle was nervous and re-looked at the presentation and her figures over, wondering what was wrong. But, everybody seemed to have liked it and the decision to progress it had been made. She went over the information over and over for the rest of the day and evening and then the next day too. She had just moved to Paris and was still finding her feet in her new role.

The meeting time came when the EA called to say he was going to be late; his previous meeting had overrun. Gabrielle took her time to compose herself and do a quick touch-up with some blush and a veil of lipstick, just as if she had just bitten her lips.

4.30 went by.

It was 4.45 when the EA called her in.

"Please sit down", as he showed her the chair on the other side of his desk. "Sorry I am late".

"It's ok," she said and couldn't think of anything else. She certainly couldn't say she was pissed off for having waited almost an hour.

They started going over the figures for the budget, and the phasing of those figures and time seemed to get by quickly when there was a knock at the door.

"Monsieur, I'm going home. Do you need anything?" his EA said.

"No, it's all right, thank you. Have a nice evening".

Gabrielle hadn't realised they had been talking for over two hours, and it was now almost seven p.m., and they were the only ones left in the office.

He stood up by the window, looking at the lit *Tour Eiffel*.

Gabrielle stood silently, not quite knowing what to do or say.

"You can see most of Paris from here. Beautiful, isn't it?"

He said, turning to look at her.

"Yes, it is",

She replied, thinking how banal her response was, 'Yes, it is. Couldn't I have said something more interesting?'

He turned his back again and continued to look outside. She wasn't sure if that was an invitation to join him. She decided it was. He wasn't looking like he wanted to return and continue talking business.

· · ·

She started walking towards him slowly, unsure if it was the right thing on many levels. As she was moving forward, he turned and looked at her intensely, savouring her every move.

Today was the day; he couldn't hold his feelings any longer. He had to know if she felt the same.

Now.

"You are beautiful",

He said, thinking how stupid and how vulnerable he was making himself right now. She could complain.

Worse, she could reject him. But he couldn't wait another minute.

He had to know.

"I have been unable to stop thinking about you; I just wanted to see you alone. Sorry for keeping you at work late",

He whispered.

Gabrielle didn't know how to react. The feminist in her should have felt at least some indignation, but she didn't. The moralist in her should have been repelled, but she wasn't. Instead, she just wanted to...

And then he kissed her. Slowly and gently at first.

Her forehead, her cheeks and then her mouth. A moment suspended in time. Or so it seemed.

Hours spent kissing. They finally walked out of the office

around nine o'clock. He walked her home, up to her door, and kissed her goodnight.

Gabrielle couldn't sleep that night. He had bypassed her barriers and gone straight to her core.

She tossed and turned and then watched the sun rise.

She was excited to go to work and took particular care in getting ready and found herself skipping down the pavement.

Gabrielle couldn't wait to see *Le PDG* again. When she arrived at the office, the door was shut, and the light was off.

"Strange", she thought.

Hours went by, and nothing.

No sign of *Le PDG.*

She heard in passing that he was travelling out of the country for an acquisition, and he won't be back until the following week. Gabrielle felt her face becoming red and had to go and collect herself.

"Stupid, stupid, did you think that he was going to tell you?"

She said, looking in the mirror.

. . .

Nevertheless, tears started to fill up her eyes. She took some time before returning to her desk and then shut the door for the rest of the day.

The week passed by slowly and uneventfully. Gabrielle was still decorating her new Paris apartment. She had decided not to sell her London home and was commuting each weekend. Going back to London was just what she needed right now; she couldn't face her empty Paris apartment, alone.

The following week came by, and her diary was filled with meetings with various board members, other directors and *Le PDG*. She couldn't help but feel anger and resentment rising, the genie was out of the bottle now, and she was struggling to put her back.

They saw each other several times with other people, and she caught him staring at her when the others weren't looking.

However, he had made no effort to contact her outside work or see her alone. Gabrielle was thinking she was delusional, that she had imagined the whole thing, until …

Until they met again. This time alone.

"How are you?" he asked.

"Fine",

She said sternly, "How can I help?"

As if nothing had happened. But it had. He drew closer and closer until their bodies touched.

"I missed you", he said

"I didn't want to miss you. I was trying not to. But I did", he whispered in her ear.

"Did you miss me?"

"Nope"

"Not even a little bit?"

He started kissing her. "Gabrielle, baby, say something".

She wanted to push him away but couldn't resist him. She kissed him back. They soon were all over each other, on his desk, by the window. He had locked the door, but people knew better than disturbing when he was in meetings.

From then on, they grabbed every moment they could.

Anywhere and everywhere during the day. And in the evenings, cooking and making love in her apartment.

They ached for each other.

Their passion was a spectacular affirmation of two minds struggling past their incongruences and inability to consistently meet their core needs in a way that was aligned with their values.

But she had violated her moral compass and now it was back to haunt her.

Paris Toujours Paris.

THE NINE LIVES OF GABRIELLE: FOR
THREE SHE STRAYS - BOOK 2

ME MYSELF and Us

LAURA MARIANI

" 'WHAT ARE YOU AFRAID OF?' HE ASKED.

'LOSING CONTROL.' I REPLIED.

'SOMETIMES LOSING CONTROL CAN BE WICKED AWESOME.' HE

SAID.

' AND SOMETIMES IT'S A DISASTER.'""

- WORDSAREPUREMAGIC

Gabrielle was standing in front of Mr Wonderful, looking at him looking at her. He was sitting at her desk by the window with a letter unfolded in his hands.

Gone was the loving look he had when she left for her walk.

The colour had drained from his cheeks. Instead, he looked stone-faced, almost grey; his eyes were red and swollen.

She couldn't understand what had happened in such a short time when she suddenly noticed the open drawer where she kept THE letter from *Le PDG*.

Before meeting *Le PDG*, Gabrielle was a provincial middle-class girl who, against the odds, had made it in the oppressively male-dominated world.

He opened her up to sexual and emotional freedom she had never before experienced.

But, this time, she was the other woman, breaking her values to meet her needs.

After her New York trip, Paris promised more freedom.
Instead, it raised more bonds to break ...

"Dear Gabrielle,

Don't be afraid of how much I desire you. I will shield you with love the next time I see you, with kisses and caresses.

I want to dive with you in all the pleasures of the flesh so that you faint.

I want you to be astounded by me and admit that you have never dreamed of such a thing possible …

And then, when you are old, I want you to remember and tremble with pleasure when you think of me.

You make me hotter than hell... everything you do gets me hotter than hell.

You have raised new hope and fun in me, and I love you, your pussy hair I felt with my fingers, the inside of your pussy, hot and wet I felt with my fingers…

All this madness I asked of you, I know there is confusion in your silence — but there are no actual words to describe my great love.…

Last night I dreamed about you; I do not know what occurred exactly. What I do know is that we kept fusing into one another. I was you. You were me.

Then, we caught fire. I remember I was smothering the fire with my shirt. But you were a different, a shadow, as drawn with chalk, and you were lifeless, fading away from me.

Please don't leave me, my darling Gabrielle. I am nothing without you."

Her cheeks went bright red, not knowing what to say. Sheepishly, she hoped that he hadn't read that far or couldn't quite grasp what the letter said. After all, Mr Wonderful's French was pretty basic …

But the look on his face told otherwise: somehow, he managed it and undoubtedly got the gist. He was sitting there, motionless and speechless. He didn't greet or hug her as he usually would have.

She knew she was in trouble. Paris, Toujours, Paris still taunting her.

Le PDG wrote that letter to her when he feared that their love affair would end soon.

It happened just after the annual Global strategy conference in *Londrienne*.

All board directors of the different companies worldwide attend the meeting as it is customs. *Le PDG* had kept the company headquarters there, just where his grandfather founded it.

The Group had now reached such a humongous proportion that they were struggling to find rooms for everyone in the only three hotels in the small town.

Many were staying in the adjacent cities, and buses had to be arranged to transport people back and forward to the three days conference. Same for the taxis: there were only two privately owned ones in town, and her PA booked one for her way in advance to ensure she could get around.

"*Bonjour Madame*", the taxi driver greeted her.

"*Nous sommes occupés, très occupés. Tout le monde et sa sœur sont venus au Vatican pour voir le Pape*", he said smiling, making the comparison between the company and *Le PDG* and Vatican City and the Pope.

This town reminded her of her childhood: her *Mamie* was French and had a house in a small village in Provence.

So Gabrielle and her parents used to spend every summer there. Although the two towns were in opposite directions, one in the North and the other in the south of France, the similarities were striking, as with most small French villages.

The love of a long mid-afternoon break and a slower pace of life is perhaps one of the reasons why living in France sounds idyllic to everybody outside France who wants to leave the city frenzy behind.

The pint-size suburb, however, made Gabrielle feel even smaller. Always did.

"Come to think of it," she thought, "the same could be said for the English place I grew up in".

Different country, same cage.

. . .

When she moved to London, it was like shredding too tight-fitting skin.

She was glad the her role was based in Paris rather than in *Londrienne*. There were only 10,000 inhabitants, one cinema and one theatre: she would go crazy living there. Moreover, everybody knew everybody; most people in town worked for the company or were connected with it.

When she was little, Paris was her dream city, and now she enjoyed the London-Paris Monday to Friday exchange.

There were some definite pluses of living in Paris: for example, even on basic salaries, you can afford to eat at *chich cafes*, try new dishes and chat for hours, a champagne lifestyle on a lemonade budget, so to speak.

She was renting a one-bedroom flat in the centre of Paris, just a few minutes from *Gare du Nord* railway station.

It overlooked some hot new restaurants in town, with lots of mismatched furniture, ping-pong tables, fantastic art and an impressive courtyard. She could watch some of the Paris hipsters milling around while cooking.

. . .

The flat was beautiful with floor-to-ceiling windows and white walls, yet rent was cheaper than in London, helping to absorb the cost of her commute.

Every Monday morning, she would get up at 6 am in London to catch the 7 am train to Paris.

She discovered that by booking her Eurostar tickets three months in advance, she could get them for € 69 in return, not much more than double a weekly travel card in London.

She would get into the *Gare du Nord* just after 10.30 am, and after a few minutes on the *Metro*, she would be in the office.

From Monday to Thursday night, she would stay at the Paris apartment and keep her work wardrobe there to save on packing. By Friday afternoon, she was ready to return to London life.

Unlike on the Tube, nobody pushes past you on the *Metro*, which also always seemed to work. Being stressed and rushed is not the Parisian thing to do. Instead, you take time to admire the surroundings and taste the *café crème*.

Overall, Gabrielle was amazed at how straightforward this arrangement had been. Her mother was upset she was further away, while her father, far more laid back, was happy whatever she was doing.

· · ·

Her London friends found it more difficult because she had minimal time to spend with them.

Living in two cities wasn't tough if it weren't for *Le PDG*.

She had travelled from Paris with the *TGV* for the annual Global conference; many others were doing the same.

The *TGV*, even first-class, was surprisingly cheap compared to railway ticket prices in the UK. It felt like the company had taken over the train.

Gabrielle had been working closely for months with the various people organising the event as part of her new branding strategy. Everything was planned for the millisecond.

She was anxious about seeing *Le PDG* with everybody there.

She had been practising her professional face in front of the mirror because she didn't trust herself. Her feelings for him. And his wife would be there. AND his children were attending the informal dinner.

Gabrielle was trying not to think about it.
     And then it happened, just like that.

· · ·

She was going over the last-minute details with the events team in the main conference room when she felt the need to turn around.

There they were: *Le PDG* and his wife.

He was showing her around, explaining the order of the day and evening, and making her feel comfortable. But, of course, she had to have her "game on", the dutiful supportive wife of the dazzling *Président* of the company.

Nathalie was tall, slender, and blonde, with long straight hair, dressed too old for her age. They had been childhood sweethearts, and she was only in her early forties.

Le PDG noticed Gabrielle was there and moved toward her to introduce them. He didn't want to, but he had to. He had just introduced *Nathalie* to everyone else in the room and couldn't avoid Gabrielle.

"How do you do?" *Nathalie* said in a charming accented English.
    The two women shook hands. Her grip was firm, resolute as to say,
    'I know who you are, and it won't make any difference. He will never leave me'.

Maybe she was, or perhaps it was Gabrielle's paranoia and jealousy. She had no right to feel jealous. She was the mistress.

· · ·

"What a difference from before ..." she thought.

She found out she was the bit on the side six months after she had split up with The Stud, after coming across a charity website that showed the picture of a couple who had a very successful fundraising event-

The Stud and his girlfriend.

The problem was that the fundraising event occurred when Gabrielle and The Stud were, allegedly, still together.

She had been the other woman, unknowingly and unwillingly so.

Gabrielle was S-I-C-K sitting in her bath, scrubbing and scrubbing for hours until she felt clean and remotely better.

She was so mad that she even dreamed of killing him a few times in the most painful way, then downgraded it to chopping his dick off.

But, THIS time, she was the other woman, knowingly and willingly.

And she experienced jealousy like never before. This time, she dreamed of killing the wife instead. Not him. Never him. He had made her feel alive like never before.

· · ·

Before leaving the room, they talked a bit longer about the order of events. After that, the rest of the day was a blur. Gabrielle ran on autopilot.

She didn't see *Le PDG* again until the evening, at dinner. She took her time and care to prepare for the evening; she wanted to dazzle him.

Make him see she was the one.

She picked a little black dress, caressing her body in all the right places, revealing her slender but curvy frame.

"You are the curviest skinny girl I have ever seen", he told her once. "I love your ass".

He was a bum man, definitely a bum man.

The dress was showing off Gabrielle's assets, like the mounting of a diamond enhancing its brilliance without being too much.

"Perfect," she thought, looking at herself in the mirror.

Just a smidge of red lipstick as if she had bitten on her lips, and she was ready to go.

· · ·

Her table was next to the main one where *Le PDG* was sitting with his wife, brother and sister and the other members of the main Board.

Gabrielle noticed he seemed distracted. He conversed politely at the table but kept turning and looking at her. He could not stop.

He wanted her, right here, right now. After that, he didn't care about anything else.

And when Gabrielle left her table to go to the ladies' room, he followed her there.

"You looked beautiful", he said.
     "I want you" as he pulled her into one of the empty rooms down the corridor and locked the door behind them.

"I want you. This is torture", *Le PDG* whispered.

"We can't. It's too dangerous," she said.

"I don't care". And, at that moment, he didn't.

He had had several liaisons before, but nothing like this. They were just unattached sex.

.   .   .

His wife tolerated his indiscretions as long as he didn't embarrass himself publicly. She knew he'd never leave her.

But this time, even *Nathalie* could sense something was different.

He had stopped his regular evening calls during the week and was distracted when they were together at the weekend. He seemed to come alive only when seeing the children and when it was time to return to Paris.

And he had started going back earlier and earlier.

He used to take the first TGV on Monday mornings. Then, it became Sunday evenings. And now he couldn't wait to leave just after Sunday lunch.

Nathalie knew something was wrong but didn't know what she could do.

Sex had never been her thing, and she was glad he had bothered less and less as the years went by. Travelling wasn't on top of her list either. She didn't have his intellectual capacity or depth and they didn't share many interests.

She knew instinctively Gabrielle was His One. She had to stop this.

· · ·

Gabrielle could hear people passing by in the corridor outside. The fear of being found out added to the excitement of being in his arms. They had to be quick because he was due to make his speech soon.

They composed themselves and left the room one at a time. She waited a few minutes before returning to the main room; checked herself in her mirror, trying to catch her breath.

She got back to her table just in time to hear him speak.

After dinner, everyone mingled and chit-chatted away; Gabrielle played her part and circulated the room, ensuring everyone was all right.

"He looks so handsome", she heard someone say. It was a group of women working in the head office from the communication department.

"I'm wondering who is he screwing now? Poor *Nathalie*", one of them said.

"I bet she lost count"; they all nodded.

"I think he is seeing *la Directrice* des Ressources Humaines right now, or so I have heard", she added.

• • •

"I'm one of the other other other women", Gabrielle stood there incredulous.

He opened her up to sexual and emotional freedom she had never before experienced. But, despite his claims to her being the woman in his life, that did not imply she had been the only one either.

She wondered how many had been before — even worse if there was someone else now.

Le PDG suddenly appeared from right behind them. The four gossiping women looked partly in shock, mortified and, most of all, terrified. *Le PDG* had heard them. They disassembled and left with their tail between their legs.

Gabrielle noticed something else, though:
    HE was the one looking terrified.

Not of what people were saying about him but of what Gabrielle was thinking. He could see it in her face. Her beautiful face was now turning away from him.

"Gabrielle, please don't leave", he said.

She couldn't bear to look at him and slowly but surely walked away. He could feel he was losing her, right there.

· · ·

They didn't talk for the rest of the evening. Then, finally, Gabrielle made her excuses and left early. The event team had everything under control, and no one needed her.

But him.

Right now, though, she didn't care. She returned to her hotel room and lay there, staring at the ceiling for hours. Her mobile phone was buzzing from the myriad of texts and voice mails he had left.

Gabrielle couldn't talk to him. Neither did she want to.

"What have I left myself into?" she thought.
"Why did I ...?

The next day was the conference's second day, and she would have called in sick if she could.

But she had commitments, so she put on a brave face and carried on as normally as possible. She avoided being in the same room alone with him as much as feasible.

Le PDG, on the other hand, wanted to be alone with Gabrielle.
Desperately.

He had to explain. Yes, there had been many before her. But they were just sex. There wasn't anybody else right now. There hadn't been anybody else since her.

. . .

Not since he first saw her, even before they had started being together.

He had to explain. Gabrielle had to know.

It was then when he wrote THE letter; he poured his heart and soul on paper.

" .... All this madness I asked of you, I know there is confusion in your silence — but there are no actual words to describe my great love....

Last night I dreamed about you .... We kept fusing into one another. I was you. You were me.

... But you were a different, a shadow, as drawn with chalk, and you were lifeless, fading away from me.

Please don't leave me, my darling Gabrielle. I am nothing without you.

I'm yours forever."

"Yes, forever mine, forever hers", she thought at the time.

And now *Le PDG* was standing between her and the most amazingly perfect man she had ever met. Loving, open, available physically and emotionally, present and tender.

· · ·

Now she was the one who had to explain to Mr Wonderful. Desperately.

"How to explain what *Le PDG* had meant to her and why?" she wasn't even sure she knew herself to the full extent.

One thing was for sure. He had to know there wasn't anybody else right now. And there hadn't been anybody else since him. Or ever will.

Me, myself and us.

AFTERWORD

Intensity-seeking is an enslavement of our own perpetuation.

When we step out of the delirium of always seeking someone new, and meet the same old sad and lonely child within, our healing journey begins.

Exhausting ourselves with novelty is a defence against our deepest pain, one that we cannot outrun.

But once we stop and feel our losses, we can being our healing journey and be the authentic joyous person we were born to be.

- *Alexandra Katehakis.*

THE NINE LIVES OF GABRIELLE:
FOR THREE SHE STRAYS - BOOK 3

Freedom
over Me

LAURA MARIANI

The Global annual meeting had ended; it had been an astounding success, especially for Gabrielle.

People commented on how different this year had been, more inclusive, more fitting of a multi-billion euros global company, a leader in its field, rather than a provincial French company. Tradition and heritage had the rightful place in the strategy.

Everybody appreciated the changes and felt the company was also starting to speak their language.

It was a bittersweet victory for Gabrielle, professionally elating but personally devastating.

Le PDG tried desperately to reach her, to talk to her. He had to explain. Gabrielle had to know.

"Madame, pour Vous", the concierge said whilst she was checking out of the hotel and handed over a letter.

"Merci," she said and settled the bill.

Looking at her handwritten name on the envelope, she knew it was from him. But she didn't open it whilst on the train back to Paris, too many people she knew around.

· · ·

She was going back to London from there for a well-deserved long weekend; there, on the Eurostar, with a glass of some kind of liquor in her hand, she started reading:

"Dear Gabrielle,

Don't be afraid of how much I desire you. I will shield you with love the next time I see you, with kisses and caresses.

I want to dive with you in all the pleasures of the flesh so that you faint.

I want you to be astounded by me and admit that you have never dreamed of such things possible ...."

Tears were streaming down her cheeks.

".......You have raised new hope and fun in me, and I love you...."

"*Madame, are you OK?*" asked the very attentive server on the train. They didn't often see many people crying their hearts out in business class.

"I'm good, thank you. Thanks for asking", Gabrielle replied.

"All this madness I asked of you, I know there is confusion in your silence — but there are no actual words to describe my great love...." she continued reading.

"Last night I dreamed about you ...... I was you. You were me.

Then, we caught fire. I remember I was smothering the fire with my shirt. But you were a different, a shadow, as drawn with chalk, and you were lifeless, fading away from me.

Please don't leave me, my darling Gabrielle. I am nothing without you."

I'm yours forever."

"Yes, forever mine, forever hers", she thought. It was the longest two and half hours of her life.

She spent the next twenty-four hours in bed. She couldn't be bothered doing anything, going anywhere. *Le PDG's* letter clutched in her hands.

Gabrielle was feeling both aching for him and repulsed at the same time.

. . .

She hadn't spoken to him yet. He called her numerous times, but she didn't pick up. She let the calls go to voicemail every time. He texted her a myriad of times, and she didn't respond either.

Ring, ring …. ring ring …

Her mobile was buzzing.

"Ciao bella", the voice said "bentornata". It was Paola, her trusted friend, checking in on her.

"Hiya", Gabrielle replied. They chatted for a while, she really wanted to be left alone, but she knew her friend was trying to jerk her out of her apathy.

"Cicci, lunch on Sunday", Paola said.

It wasn't a question, and she wouldn't have taken no for an answer anyway.
    "I'll come to Islington, and we'll go somewhere in your area".

Gabrielle knew it was pointless arguing or saying no; she would have shown up at her house anyway. Paola knew how to shake her up when she needed it.

. . .

"Remember to bring your passport when you are travelling from the suburbs", Gabrielle said, with their longstanding joke about Paola living in Richmond.

"I'll try. See you Sunday", she said.

Sunday came quicker than she realised, et voilà, it was soon time to meet Paola for a good catch-up.

Paola, her no-nonsense Italian friend who she had known since she had arrived in London.

Paola managed not to lose her strong accent after almost twenty years in the country. She always made Gabrielle smile.

The weather was warming up, and they were looking for somewhere to eat with outside space. Londoners turn into mini lizards and seek the sun whenever it seems like it is coming out.

Ultimately, they opted for The Alwyne Castle, a charming pub in Islington with a beer garden, situated only a minute's walk from Highbury & Islington underground station.

The Alwyne has lots of space, especially outside, which is ideal for building a suntan and carries a good beer and wine selection.

. . .

They met for an early Sunday lunch; Gabrielle definitely needed some cheering before heading back to Paris.

"Hello ladies", said the waiter ", a table outside or inside?".
   "Outside, outside", they replied in unison.

They both glanced at the menu and quickly chose: beef carpaccio and seared scallops, perfectly done and seasoned for starter and the obligatory Sunday Roast (obviously).

"Any drinks while you are waiting?"

Gabrielle and Paola looked at each other and said, "A bottle of house red and sparkling water, thanks".

"So, *ciccia mia*, what's going on?" Paola started as soon as the waiter had left their table.

It had been a while since they last saw each other, and they had a lot to talk about.

Gabrielle, slowly and softly, started to tell her story: her first meeting with *Le PDG*, their clandestine meetings anywhere and everywhere, and, to finish, she recounted what just happened in *Londrienne* at the global annual conference.

"Seared scallops?" the server interrupted.

"Me", Paola raised her hand.

"Ciccia, ciccia, no no no ..." Paola went on after he had served them with their starters.

"But, but you are having an affair too," Gabrielle responded, baffled.

Paola had been married to an Englishman for the last ten years, and they had two gorgeous daughters. She loved them all dearly; however, she had kept her bit on the side: an Italian lover Paola met from time to time when visiting her mother every couple of months.

"*La differenza mia cara*, for me it's just sex.

I tell Marco I'm going over; if he is available, we meet; if he isn't, it is still OK, like a 'human vibrator' on call. Nothing else. He knows how to make me come, and he does his job.

He doesn't want or need anything more from me and me from him".

Her husband lacked a bit in the sex drive department and was happy to go without it. Paola wasn't.

. . .

Martin was an outstanding father and husband; she would never leave him, but needs were needs.

"Tu ciccia mia, are getting involved. No, correction, you are involved emotionally.

Plus, you feel guilty even when you find money on the pavement, or someone gives you extra change in shops. Remember that time you went back to return ten pence? Ten pence. And now you are having an affair with a married man?" she paused, shaking her head.

"No, no, no, not for you. I can read guilt splattered all over your face; it is consuming you".

The main course arrived; Gabrielle was impressed that they managed to handle the timing of the two orders with no problem, especially considering she liked her beef still muuuing and rare whilst her friend liked it almost cremated.

The beef was delicious, and the beef dripping roast potatoes were perfectly cooked.

Gabrielle knew Paola was right. But she couldn't bear to stop it yet.

. . .

"Relationships aren't easy," she thought, "they take a different take because the memories and stories can transform during crucial moments", she was illuding herself.

Finally, they ended the meal with the British Cheeseboard washed down with more red.

"*Se hai bisogno, lo sai che sono qui*", Paola said.
"I know".

At 6.00 am on Monday morning, Gabrielle started to get ready to leave the house. The first Eurostar to Paris was at 7.00 am, and St Pancras station was not that far from her home; she had plenty of time.

The two and half hours seemed to pass by incredibly slowly. It felt more like a lifetime.

On the one hand, she was glad. But, on the other hand, she wasn't really looking forward to seeing him again. Gabrielle was postponing the inevitable, and she had to meet him sometime. She was working directly for him, after all.

Until meeting *Le PDG*, Gabrielle's life experience was mainly secondhand, observed, and never viscerally involved. And now that her layers are slowly peeling away, and all the emotions she had repressed for so long, jealousy, frustration, and anger were coming to the surface.

· · ·

All her life, she had been a closet bohemian. She always loved to live big, outrageously. Outside she was the perfect daughter and businesswoman but inside, she had always been Isadora Duncan.

She wanted a life outside the bell curve and to suck the marrow out of life. But she wanted people to like her too…
And so, she conformed.

Gabrielle arrived at the office after 11.00 am. People were still buzzing from the conference; she noticed *Le PDG* was not in.

"Good", she thought. She preferred it that away, at least today.

The day went by, and she had meetings back to back, so she had no time to think.

She left the office a bit late but decided to walk home anyway. Even though it was a bit far from *Tour Montparnasse* to the right behind *Gare Du Nord,* she needed the fresh air.

When she arrived at her building, he was standing there. *Le PDG.* He was holding a bouquet of purple hyacinths in his hands, and one single red rose.

"I'm sorry", he said. "I should have told you myself. I took for granted that you knew about the gossip mill like everyone else seems to.

. . .

"I can't stop thinking about you. Please don't leave me. I am nothing without you."

And there he was, standing right in front of the building entrance; she couldn't get in without acknowledging his presence one way or the other.

She didn't want to, but she was aching for him.

"There has been no other since I met you. Only you", he continued.

"Did you get my letter?" he asked. Gabrielle nodded.

And suddenly, they were making love in her apartment, on the floor, on the table, starving for each other. They stayed up all night; it was the first time he had stayed over.

And from then on, it became more regular. Le PDG was scared of losing Gabrielle and was trying his best to reassure her.

She wasn't one of the many other women, but the other woman nevertheless.

. . .

Relationships aren't easy; they take a different take because of the memories and stories transformed during crucial moments.

Gabrielle had decided to stop commuting for a bit and fully experience Paris. At least for a while. She had to give Paris the attention and love it deserved.

"Paris is always a good idea", Audrey Hepburn said.

"Indeed, it is Audrey. Indeed it is." And even though summer in France meant a looooong holiday for the French who escaped to the coast or family house, it was worthed.

Gabrielle enjoyed walking around Paris and taking in the open-air architectural views, which were even more breath-taking with the sunshine.

"Summer brings out the best in Paris", she thought, "long days and nights when you can enjoy walking out and about, stunning views, sipping cocktails on terraces and dining al fresco".

Her Paris apartment was small and without outside space but there were many gorgeous parks in Paris she could enjoy:

big ones (*Bois de Vincennes, Bois de Boulogne, Buttes-Chaumont, Parc Floral, Parc de la Villette*),

elegant ones (*Palais-Royal, Jardin du Luxembourg, Jardins des Plantes*), and the in-between (*Parc Monceau, Parc Montsouris*).

All very charming and hosting various summer events that pair well with picnic time, and Gabrielle took full advantage of them.

Le PDG sometimes stayed at the weekend, and they relished watching the occasional movie in the *Parc de la Villette*, where there is a month-long *Cinema en Plein Air festival* with the city's most gigantic movie screen.

It was perfect, almost idyllic: some delicious food and a bottle of wine watching a movie whilst the sun set - the illusion of a proper relationship.

With or without *Le PDG* though, Gabrielle wanted to enjoy Paris, sometimes taking a tour alone from a boat on the Seine.

A tour on *Les Bateaux Mouches* lasts approximately two and six hours and offers great sightseeing with commentary with plenty of Champagne. Or a meal served on exquisite white linen.

She deserved to experience all of it.

She loved how, in the summer, Paris becomes a seaside resort and welcomes *Paris Plages* in the new *Parc Rives de Seine*, with sun loungers and palm trees popping up just by the water's edge.

Plus, every boutique and department store in Paris has super anticipated sales *soldes d'été.*

She was squeezing in as much as she could as if she knew ...

Summer came and went, and the relationship with *Le PDG* became more stable, almost routine, and predictable.

It was as if they had sucked the marrow out, and now only the bones were left behind, holding the skeleton up. Nevertheless, he was still her addiction.

Gabrielle realised that she had now been in Paris, in her position for almost a year.

"Career progression is slow in Paris", she had been thinking.
    "Somehow, people stay in the same position much longer than in the UK, where everyone expects to be promoted or move every couple of years".

She was feeling restless but wasn't quite sure why.

Her role was keeping her very busy with regular travel to the different branches of the company worldwide. Christmas was just around the corner.

She was away from the office more and more, and working from home started to creep in. From the London home.

She started commuting again and travelling back on Thursdays more regularly.

And then, just like that, everything changed ...

On Monday, 23 March 2020, the Prime Minister announced the first lockdown in the UK, ordering people to stay at home. And on 26 March, the lockdown measures legally came into force. Gabrielle was stuck in London.

Life can turn just in a second. Just like that. All the things you always wanted to do on pause. Until someone else decides to press the play button again.

Tomorrow, always longing for tomorrow, and suddenly, there almost wasn't a tomorrow.

Gabrielle kept in touch with the office, making great use of Teams and Zoom and continued working.

To be fair, she enjoyed being back in her home and the alone time.

. . .

She had always been a loner: a child lost in her books, as an adult chasing the next win in the never-ending climb.

She had cancelled many events before, dates, and meetings with friends at the last minute.

There was always tomorrow. There was always something more important to do.

But, after a while, her body and brain started fighting themselves. They were fighting her or something.

She felt exhausted all the time, and all the energy was wiped out of her. She was so fatigued that she was struggling to complete even the most minor tasks. And yet, Gabrielle was unable to get any rest.

She tested to see if she had caught the dreaded C, but no, she hadn't.

Her body was on fire. And on top of throbbing soreness, she was experiencing pins-and-needles sensation prickling throughout.

Her mind went into overdrive to the point where she was feeling paranoid, irritable and moody. She couldn't stay still for even a moment.

She couldn't understand what was happening to her.

After a few months, with the physical symptoms subsiding, she was starting to see things clearly again.

She had been withdrawing from the most potent drug.

Overall, the various lockdowns and consequent restrictions had been good for her, a time to focus on herself with little distraction.

And now, after the 'detox', she was getting to know who Gabrielle actually was or wanted to be.

Fully and unapologetically. Isadora Duncan and all.
    And levelling up big time.

The pandemic gave Gabrielle a new, more in-depth appreciation of being out there, alone, in gratitude for life. Appreciating everything that she was so lucky to be able to experience.

Sometimes it takes a great emergency or crisis to delve deep and discover how much more you can do. Or should do.

· · ·

Gabrielle had never been afraid to make big choices: she left her big corporate job, Paris and *Le PDG*, in the middle of the pandemic.

Everybody thought she was crazy. But she knew it was the right thing to do.

She wanted to take her time to figure out what she really wanted. And so she reconnected with her inner Isadora and reprised some childhood passion, and started writing and illustrating children's books and a YouTube channel/ podcast.

She also began to treat her body and herself with more love and kindness, no more torture and self-flagellation with super hard schedules. Or self-destructive affairs. Nothing left to prove.

She liked this Gabrielle. And this Gabrielle had attracted the most wonderful man.

She had to make sure that Mr Wonderful knew that THE letter he was holding in his hands was only a page in the book of her life, a chapter fully closed, and she was waiting to continue writing her story with him, and only him.

For Gabrielle had played, had strayed,
    and now she was ready to stay.

… Because the greatest love of all
Is happening to me
I found the greatest love of all
Inside of me
The greatest love of all
Is easy to achieve
Learning to love yourself
It is the greatest love of all

---

songwriters: **Linda Creed , Michael Masser**

DISCLAIMER

The Nine Lives of Gabrielle: For Three She Strays is a work of fiction.

Although its form is that of an autobiography, Gabrielle's, it is not one.

With the exception of public places, any resemblance to persons living or dead is coincidental. Space and time have been rearranged to suit the convenience of the book, memory has its own story to tell.

The opinions expressed are those of the characters and should not be confused with the author's.

AUTHOR'S NOTE

Thank you so much for reading *The Nine Lives of Gabrielle: For Three She Strays.*

I hope you enjoyed this novellas as a form of escapism, but perhaps you also glimpsed something beneath as you read. A review would be much appreciated as it helps other readers discover the story. Thanks.

If you sign up for my newsletter you'll be notified of giveaways, new releases and receive personal updates from behind the scenes of my business and books.

Go to www.thepeoplealchemist.com to get started.

Places in the book

I have set the story in real places in Paris and in a modelled fictional town in the north of France for *Le PDG* backstory. You can see some of the places/mentions here:

- Bois de Vincennes

- Bois de Boulogne,
- Buttes-Chaumont
- Canonbury Square and Gardens
- Cinema en Plein Air festival
- Eurostar
- Gare du Nord
- Highbury & Islington
- Jardin du Luxembourg
- Jardins des Plantes
- Le Metro
- Parc Rives de Seine
- Paris Plages
- Parc Floral
- Parc de la Villette Palais-Royal
- Parc Monceau
- Parc Montsouris
- TGV (train à grande vitesse)
- The Alwyne Castle
- Tour Eiffel
- Tour Montparnasse

Bibliography

I read different books as part of my research. Some of them together with other references include:

The Artist Way - **Julia Cameron**

The Complete Reader - **Neville Goddard**, compiled and edited by **David Allen**

Psycho-Cybernetics - **Maxwell Maltz**

A Theory of Human Motivation - **Abraham Maslow**

Printed in Great Britain
by Amazon